Dear Reader:

Here is a book that is pure pleasure to read.

If you like this kind of fantasy book (it could never really happen, but wouldn't it be great if it did?) and want to read more about Warton and his escapades, you may want to check out other books by Russell Erickson, such as *A Toad for Tuesday, Warton & Morton,* and *Warton & the King of the Skies* in your school or town library.

While this was very popular when it was first published, *Warton & the Traders* is now out of print. So you can buy this book only through the Weekly Reader Book Club. We like to keep the best books for kids around, even if it means publishing them ourselves.

We hope you enjoy this book as much as we do.

Sincerely,

Stephen Fraser

Stephen Fraser
Senior Editor
Weekly Reader Books

Weekly Reader Book Club Presents

WARTON AND THE TRADERS

by RUSSELL E. ERICKSON

pictures by
LAWRENCE DI FIORI

This book is a presentation of Newfield Publications, Inc. Newfield Publications offers book clubs for children from preschool through high school. For further information write to: **Newfield Publications, Inc.,** 4343 Equity Drive, Columbus, Ohio 43228.

Published by arrangement with Russell E. Erickson and Lawrence DiFiori. Originally published by Lothrop, Lee & Shepard Company, a division of William Morrow & Company, Inc. Newfield Publications is a trademark of Newfield Publications, Inc. Weekly Reader is a federally registered trademark of Weekly Reader Corporation.

Library of Congress Cataloging in Publication Data
Erickson, Russell E.
    Warton and the traders
SUMMARY: Warton Toad turns the wood rats' trading habits to his own advantage by agreeing to help them trap the dreaded wildcat in exchange for their assistance in rescuing a starving fawn.
    [1. Toads—Fiction. 2. Animals—Fiction]
I. Di Fiori, Lawrence. II. Title.
PZ7.E2757Wash   [E]   78-25689
ISBN 0-688-41886-4   ISBN 0-688-51886-9 lib. bdg.
            Printed in the United States of America.
First Edition   2 3 4 5 6 7 8 9 10

WARTON
AND THE
TRADERS

Among the vast evergreens, which stretched farther than any eye could see, there appeared scattered spots of crimson, and yellow, and brown. And, although the days were still bright and warm, the nights yet soft and pleasant, there could be no denying the fact that another fall had come to the deep forest.

For the two toad brothers, Warton and Morton, it was a time of year when there was much to do in their cozy underground home. For Warton, besides his usual cleaning chores, there were cracks to plug and repairs to be made. For Morton, besides his usual cooking chores, there was canning and preserving to be done.

There was also a certain trip to be made, and Warton had just gotten ready for it. Wearing his corduroy pants, his green sweater with four gold buttons, his flat cap, and his walking boots, he stepped into the kitchen.

"I'm all set to leave for Aunt Toolia's," he shouted over the sound of clattering jars and boiling kettles.

"That's good!" yelled Morton, who was standing at the stove amid swirling clouds of steam.

Warton went to the kitchen table, where five sparkling clean jars stood in a row. He smacked his lips as he read their labels. "Gnat Relish! Caterpillar Chili! Pickled Dragonflies! And here's Aunt Toolia's favorite ... Sweet and Sour Snails!"

Morton set a pot in the sink, and then stood beside Warton. "Exactly what I send her every year," he said proudly.

"Right," said Warton. "And when I return, I'll be bringing one jar of Aunt Toolia's gooseberry marmalade, one jar of grape ketchup, one jar of rhubarb jam, and two jars of her delicious spiced moth eggs."

Morton nodded. "Exactly what *she* sends us every year."

Warton carefully put the jars into his traveling pack. When he was finished, Morton handed him a small bag.

"It's a lunch for along the way," said Morton, hurrying back to his stove. "And remember," he warned as he lifted a lid from a rumbling kettle, "be as careful as you can."

"I will," promised Warton, putting on his pack. He said good-bye, and went up a tunnel that came out at the bottom of an old stump. There he turned to the south, and he was on his way to Aunt Toolia's.

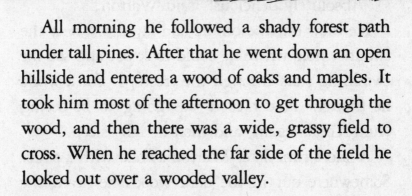

All morning he followed a shady forest path under tall pines. After that he went down an open hillside and entered a wood of oaks and maples. It took him most of the afternoon to get through the wood, and then there was a wide, grassy field to cross. When he reached the far side of the field he looked out over a wooded valley.

Warton started downwards. Seeing how long the shadows had become, he suddenly realized that the day was nearly done. He traveled on, but the light faded quickly, and when darkness came he found himself in a hollow, deep in the valley. He knew he must find a place to spend the night, and he hopped into a hole at the bottom of a dead tree.

"This will be perfect!" he said. "I'll sleep here and be on my way first thing in the morning."

As soon as Warton took off his pack he lit a candle. Its warm glow quickly made him feel quite safe. Next he spread out his blanket. Then he unwrapped his lunch and ate two deviled snail sandwiches and drank two cups of black cherry tea.

"Absolutely delicious!" said Warton.

He blew out the candle and lay down near the entrance hole where he could look out and see the twinkling stars through the treetops. For a while he thought how nice it was going to be seeing Aunt Toolia again, and then he fell asleep.

A short time later Warton awoke with a start. Somewhere out in the dark woods he heard the rustling of dry leaves. When he held his breath to listen, the sound stopped. When he began to breathe again, the rustling sound started anew. This time it was louder.

All at once a horrible scream echoed throughout the valley. It was the most ghastly sound Warton had ever heard. He sprang to his feet and, pressing himself against the side of the entrance hole, he peered into the night.

As he did, the terrible scream came again and Warton saw a large, dark shape bounding with great speed between the moonlit trees. He was wondering what the creature could be after when he saw two much smaller shapes scurrying over the woodland floor a short distance away.

"Over here, hurry!" Warton cried out.

The words were no sooner out of his mouth when he knew he might have done a very foolish thing. He hadn't the slightest idea what the smaller creatures were. For all he knew, they might be toad-eaters.

But it was too late. There was a scuffling in the fallen leaves, the two shadowy figures turned

11

sharply and, one behind the other, they dashed into the hollow tree.

For a moment there was nothing but the sound of heavy breathing. Then came a thunderous roar, and the tree shuddered as the creature outside flung itself against the trunk.

"What kind of animal is that?" cried Warton.

From the darkness beside him a frightened voice answered, "It's ... it's a wildcat!"

Warton heard a low snarling and the scratching of wood as the wildcat searched for a way to get in. Suddenly a large eye peered in through the entrance hole. It shimmered yellow-green in the moonlight and turned slowly from side to side. There was a loud hiss as a thick paw shot into the tree. Sharp claws narrowly missed Warton's head, and he jumped back.

Then the wildcat dug his paw into the soft earth, and with a low growl pulled a pile of dirt outside the tree. He reached into the tree again, and again he pulled out a pile of dirt.

Warton watched horrified as the entrance hole began to grow larger. A few more scoops, and the

wildcat would be able to get into the tree with ease.

But then there came the sound of sharp claws raking across hard stone. The wildcat had struck a boulder and could dig no farther. He let out a scream of rage and, hissing and spitting, he clawed at the bark of the tree till the sound inside was deafening. He gave one more terrible cry. There was a stirring in the leaves ... and he was gone.

Warton let out a long sigh. "I wonder if he'll be back."

"Not tonight," said a voice in the darkness. "He'll just go after someone else."

Although Warton was relieved that the wildcat

would not be back, he was beginning to feel nervous about being in such a small place with two creatures he knew nothing about.

"Perhaps," he thought, "I'd better get close to the entrance, just in case." He moved slowly toward the dim light of the entrance hole when, all at once, a dark object appeared there. Warton gulped as he realized one of the creatures was now standing in his way.

"Do I smell a candle?" said a voice.

"Yes," Warton said. "It's mine."

"Why don't you light it?" said the voice.

Warton knew he couldn't refuse. As soon as he located the candle he put a match to it. The flame fluttered and as the hollow tree filled with a soft, reddish light, he saw animals he had never seen before. Their thick fur, which went right to the tips of their tails, was a rich brown, except on their stomachs, where it was pure white. Their ears were small and pointed. Their eyes were round and black.

"We're wood rats," said the one near the entrance, as he noticed Warton's stare. He was brushing the dust from his clothes. First he did his leather boots, then his neatly pressed knickers, then his white short-sleeved shirt, and finally his red vest.

Warton turned to look at the other wood rat. He was quite a bit larger than the first, and as he sat with his back against the inside of the tree trunk, he seemed not to have a care in the world. His plaid pants were baggy. His orange suspenders were frayed. His tie, which he wore although he had no shirt, was wrinkled. His hat was crumpled.

Both wood rats, Warton noticed, had large white sacks beside them.

As soon as the smaller rat was dusted off, he went over to Warton. "My name's Higg," he said, "and my friend's name is Bundy."

"Mine's Warton," said Warton.

"We owe you our lives," said Higg, opening his sack. He poked about a bit and pulled out a green lampshade. "Here," he said, "take it."

"Oh, no," said Warton, startled. "I don't want that."

16

Higg looked disappointed. "Well, maybe I have something you'll like better," he said, searching in his sack again.

"Please don't bother," said Warton.

"But you don't understand," said Higg. "You did us a favor—you must let us give you something in return."

Warton could see that it was very important to Higg that he accept a gift. "All right," he said. "I'll take the lampshade."

Higg immediately brightened up, and handed the lampshade to Warton. When Bundy saw that, he brought out a pair of scissors, and with a shrug Warton accepted them also.

"Good," said Higg happily. "And now that that's taken care of, tell us, Warton, how long have you lived in this tree?"

"Oh, I don't live here," replied Warton. "I'm just spending the night."

"Aha," said Higg. "Then perhaps you wouldn't mind if Bundy and I stay here also. It will be safer for us to return home tomorrow."

"I wouldn't mind at all," said Warton. "But do

18

you mean you don't live here in the valley?"

"No, no," laughed Higg. "We're here on business."

"We're traders," spoke up Bundy.

"That's right," said Higg. "When we heard of a new squirrel family that moved into this valley, we came to see what they had to trade."

"It was a waste of time," said Bundy.

"Quite true," agreed Higg. "They had nothing worth the bother of climbing all the way to the top of an oak tree for. Then, to make matters worse, that wildcat sprang on us as we were returning home to The Bog."

"The Bog?" said Warton, his eyes wide. Although he had never been there, he had often heard that it was a terrible place—a place of oozy mud and slimy moss, a place where giant snakes slithered through mucky waters, and bats fluttered in dark skies. "You live in The Bog?" he said.

Higg nodded. "Most everyone is afraid of The Bog," he said, "but once one learns its ways—such as where to go, and especially where *not* to go—it's a fine place."

19

Bundy was smiling wistfully. "I love The Bog," he said. Then suddenly he frowned. "I wish that wildcat hadn't come there four days ago, though. He's eating all our friends."

When Bundy said that, Higg too looked glum.

It bothered Warton to see the wood rats so depressed, and he grabbed his pack. He took out his last deviled snail sandwich and offered half to each rat, hoping it might cheer them up.

Bundy ate his half quickly, and as soon as he was finished he reached into his sack and brought out a tack hammer. "For the sandwich," he said, offering it to Warton.

Before Warton could say anything, Higg pre-

sented him with a teacup. Warton looked at the rats awaiting his approval. He knew it would only hurt their feelings if he didn't accept. "Thank you," he said.

The rats seemed delighted.

"And now, for something different," said Higg, opening his sack again. Tenderly he brought out a highly polished bugle.

"Do you play?" asked Warton.

Higg nodded. Then, with a bit of a flourish, he raised the instrument to his mouth.

Warton settled back to await the music. The first note was somewhat shrill and faltering, and he decided Higg was only warming up. But then more notes came forth, and they were even worse than the first. Warton realized Higg hadn't been warming up at all. He was playing with all his heart, and he was an absolutely terrible bugle player.

The inside of the tree soon was vibrating with shrieking high notes and croaking low notes. As Higg played on, his eyes grew bright and he seemed completely inspired.

21

After a while Warton's head was ringing, and for some strange reason his toes were becoming numb.

At last Higg stopped. Looking very pleased with himself, he turned towards Warton. "What better way to relax," he said, patting his bugle.

Bundy, who had been sitting quietly all the time, looked at Warton. "Don't you just love good music?" he said.

"I... I do," said Warton, his head still ringing.

"Thank you," said Higg. "But I'm afraid it's too late for me to play anymore. We should get our sleep."

Quickly Warton blew out the candle before Higg could change his mind.

Everyone said good night, and soon the toad and the two wood rats were sleeping peacefully.

When Warton awoke next morning, the wood rats were snoring loudly, and beams of sunlight streamed through the entrance hole.

"It's late," he thought, jumping up. "I'd better be going."

Not wishing to disturb the slumbering rats, he packed his things and went outside to have his breakfast. Sitting on a flat rock, he contentedly ate two carrotfly muffins with honeysuckle jelly. Then he drank the last of the tea, which was nearly cold, and was on his way.

The valley was soon behind him, and as he got closer to Aunt Toolia's his pace quickened. Then, in the early afternoon, he was there. He had come to the top of a sunny hillside, and below him lay hundreds of blueberry bushes, their leaves now the fiery red of autumn. At the bottom of the hill, rising from a patch of ferns, was the familiar white birch that arched gracefully over Aunt Toolia's home.

Warton hurried down the hill, taking the shortcut that passed between Aunt Toolia's two gardens. He stopped suddenly, studying first the flower garden and then the vegetable garden. Both were badly in need of weeding. Many of the vegetables were overripe.

"That's strange," thought Warton, moving on towards the house. "I've never seen her gardens look like this before. She usually tends them every day."

He knocked on a round wooden door set into the roots of the birch tree, and waited for Aunt Toolia's familiar voice to answer. But no sound came from within. He knocked again, harder this time, and slowly the door swung open.

With a big grin Warton jumped inside. "Surprise!" he shouted.

But Aunt Toolia wasn't there. And as Warton looked about, it was he who was surprised. Never had he seen the little home look like this. Instead of being neat and spotlessly clean—for Aunt Toolia was an even more fastidious housekeeper than Warton—it was a mess. There was dust on

everything. There were dishes in the sink. There were half-made cookies on the table. There was an overturned washtub in the middle of the floor, and red stains were spattered over everything.

Warton removed his pack, and started searching the other rooms. But Aunt Toolia was nowhere to be seen. Then, as he stood in the parlor, he noticed a peculiar silence. He looked at the wall and was shocked to see that the pendulum of the cuckoo clock, which Aunt Toolia always wound faithfully, was hanging still.

"Something's happened to Aunt Toolia!" he cried.

26

He rushed outside and headed straight for Aunt Toolia's nearest neighbors—two woodchucks named Olga and Gustave. Halfway up a sandy hillside he found Gustave lying on his back enjoying the afternoon sun.

"Gustave, wake up!" cried Warton.

The woodchuck blinked his eyes in the sunlight. "Oh hello, Morton," he said lazily. "How are you today?"

"I'm fine," replied Warton, not bothering to correct the woodchuck. "Do you know what happened to Aunt Toolia?"

"No," said Gustave. "Tell me about it."

"I mean, I don't know where she is," said Warton.

"Oh," said the drowsy woodchuck. "Well then, let's go inside and ask Olga. I'm sure she can tell you." Gustave tried to get up, but he had grown very fat in preparation for winter, and could only flop about.

"I could go ask her myself," offered Warton.

"Thank you," said Gustave, with a sigh of relief.

Warton followed a passageway deep into the hillside till he entered a tidy kitchen.

"Why, Warton, what a nice surprise," said Olga, who was stirring a pot of corncob chowder. She filled a bowl and handed it to Warton.

Although he wasn't hungry, Warton took the chowder, just to be polite. "Do you know what's happened to Aunt Toolia?" he asked.

"Hmmmph!" said Olga as she waddled to a chair. "Your Aunt Toolia has become very inconsiderate! That's what's happened to her! She promised to bake three dozen of her special cookies for Gustave's birthday. Well, his birthday was four days ago, and she hasn't come by yet!"

Warton nearly spilled his chowder. "Four days ago!" he exclaimed. "Then I must be going right away!"

With Olga staring after him, Warton dashed back outside. He jumped over Gustave and slid down the sandy hillside, wondering which way to go.

"I know!" he said aloud. "Lottie, Minnie, and Ramona—the chipmunk sisters!"

Warton hurried along the path till he came to a mossy log that lay wedged between some rocks. There was a small door under the log, and from behind it a constant chattering could be heard.

When Warton knocked, a high-pitched voice called, "Come in if you're good-looking." Then there was a great deal of giggling.

Warton entered the chipmunks' home. As always, he found it uncomfortably warm, and he noticed the smell of boiled radishes, a dish the chipmunks ate three times a week.

"Why, it's Warton!" said Minnie, when the toad rushed inside. She was sitting at a round table with her sisters, and all three were knitting away on a dark red bedspread.

"This is a nice surprise," said Lottie. She got up and poured Warton a cup of blueberry leaf tea. "It's just too bad your Aunt Toolia doesn't see fit to visit us anymore."

"It certainly is," said Ramona, offering some cupcakes to Warton. "After all, she did promise to do the fringe work, and now we're nearly done, and she hasn't come near us in days."

"Why, we haven't seen her in so long," said

Minnie, "it almost seems like she's vanished."

At that Lottie looked startled. "Oh, my goodness," she said, "I hope she hasn't done what Cousin Beatrice did. You remember when *she* vanished, don't you?" she said to her sisters.

"Remember?" said Minnie. "Who could forget! Imagine, running off to take gliding lessons from a flying squirrel!"

"What happened to her?" asked Warton.

"Exactly what you would expect," said Ramona. "She got killed the first time she jumped out of a tree."

Warton gulped. "Excuse me," he said. "I must go."

Once outside, Warton walked on, filled with concern for Aunt Toolia, but not knowing where to turn next. Soon he found himself under the curved canes of a blackberry thicket. Ahead the path disappeared into the shadows of the deep woods. He looked up, and the dusky sky he saw told him that night was approaching again. He turned around to start back to Aunt Toolia's empty home.

31

"Good evening," said a voice nearby.

Startled, Warton looked about and saw a whippoorwill sitting on the ground. His brown speckled feathers so closely matched the dry leaves around him, he was nearly invisible.

"Out for a stroll?" asked the bird, cocking his head.

"No," replied Warton. "I'm looking for my Aunt Toolia. I'm afraid she may be in trouble."

"Does your Aunt Toolia always carry an umbrella," said the bird, "even on sunny days?"

"Yes," said Warton. "She says it pays to be prepared for showers."

"In that case," said the bird, "she may, indeed, be in trouble."

Warton could hardly speak. "You've seen her?"

"About four days ago," said the bird. "Because of the trees, I couldn't see her very well, but I did notice that she took the north turn there where the path divides. That surprised me, I must say."

"Why?" asked Warton. "Where does it go?"

"Not to any place for a toad," answered the whippoorwill. "That path goes straight to The Bog."

"The Bog!" gasped Warton. And, as the bird told about the terrible creatures to be found there, Warton remembered the wildcat. Why, he was more powerful and more fearsome than all the others put together, and he was probably at The Bog right now!

With a worried look, Warton backed away from the whippoorwill. "Thank you for your help," he said.

"Wait!" called the bird. "If you're not careful, you'll end up at The Bog yourself!"

In the fading twilight Warton followed the path into the thick woods. When he came to a fork, he remembered what the whippoorwill had said: "She took the north turn."

After Warton had turned north, there was hardly a path at all. "It looks like no one ever goes this way," he thought. "I wonder why Aunt Toolia did?"

In a zigzagging course, he made his way up a long hill strewn with fallen trees and broken branches. Halfway down the other side he stopped and sniffed. The air was heavy and dank, and smelled of mud and rotting wood.

Farther along the path disappeared completely, and so too did the twilight. Warton looked about the dark woods that surrounded him, and then, between two trees, he saw the reflection of the rising moon glimmering on water.

"The Bog!" he said in a soft whisper.

He started for the water, but a wide patch of giant skunk cabbages lay in his way. Then, somehow, the skunk cabbages were behind him, and he stood at last on a soggy clump of moss at The Bog's edge.

The waters were still and black, the woods deathly silent. Overhead, bats fluttered in the evening sky.

Warton took a deep breath. "Aunt Toolia!" he shouted.

All was silent.

Warton shouted again. Still there was no answer, and he decided to go deeper into The Bog.

He had not gone very far when a faint sound came out of the darkness. Warton suddenly remembered that, besides being where the wildcat lived, The Bog was also the home of slithering snakes and ugly snapping turtles, and other toad-eating animals. He was searching for a place to hide when the grass in front of him moved, and it was too late.

The slender blades parted, and Warton's eyes grew wide as something appearing to have risen from the very muck itself stepped out of the grass. Trailing long pieces of moss and covered from head to foot with gobs of mud, it came towards him.

Then the creature stopped. It bent over to set down a pile of grass and twigs it carried. Warton knew this was his chance to make a jump for safety. Yet he couldn't. His eyes were glued to the creature. Somehow it seemed familiar, and when at last he saw the creature's face, he gasped.

"Aunt Toolia! Is that you?" he cried.

"Shhh," cautioned the mud-covered toad. "This is a very dangerous place." Then Aunt Toolia gave Warton a hug so tight he felt the air go right out of him. And, before he could catch his breath, she gave him another squeeze. "I've *never* been happier to see anyone in my whole life," she said. "How did you ever manage to find me here?"

As Aunt Toolia sat on her bundle of grass, Warton told her about the whippoorwill.

"My, my," said Aunt Toolia. "I'm going to bake that whippoorwill a big, juicy squashbug pie the day I leave this place."

"But can't you leave now?" said Warton. "And why did you ever come here anyway?"

"Oh, my goodness," said Aunt Toolia, picking up her bundle, "I nearly forgot. I don't have time to explain. Just follow me and you'll understand."

Aunt Toolia jumped onto one of the branches of a fallen sycamore tree. From there she jumped to the trunk, which Warton noticed lay like a bridge from the muddy shore to a tiny island of earth out in the water. When she reached the other end she jumped down and disappeared behind the tree's upturned roots.

Warton waited no longer. He too jumped onto the tree and followed along. The bark was slippery, and he had to be very careful lest he fall into the dark waters.

When he came to the end of the tree, Warton jumped off and went to look behind the high wall of roots and sod. There Aunt Toolia was giving her full attention to something down in a shallow little hollow.

Warton went cautiously closer. "Why, it's a fawn!" he exclaimed. He could hardly believe his eyes. He had seen many a young deer, but never had he seen one being cared for by a toad. It was lying on its side, and Aunt Toolia was fussing over one of its hind legs, which was propped between two sticks. Adjusting a large bandage, made from

an apron, she set her pile of grass and twigs in front of the fawn's nose.

"Here you are," she said tenderly.

The fawn looked at Aunt Toolia with the biggest and softest brown eyes Warton had ever seen. He flicked out his tongue and, in an instant, the pile was gone. He smiled weakly and shut his eyes.

"Dear me," said Aunt Toolia, "I've never seen such an appetite." She turned towards Warton. "I've been trying to take care of the poor thing ever since one horrible day last week when simply everything went wrong."

Aunt Toolia whispered so as not to wake the fawn, and as Warton listened he heard a sound like the gentle rippling of water. Then there came the crunch of small stones. He looked to the water's edge, and there looking back at him was the hideous head of a snapping turtle. On short, round legs the ugly beast moved straight towards the two toads.

Warton was about to shout a warning to Aunt Toolia when he noticed she had seen the turtle too.

He watched, astonished, as she calmly reached under a bush and pulled out her umbrella, which was bent nearly in half. Then, marching to the water's edge, Aunt Toolia gave the umbrella a swing, and there was a dull thud as she hit the turtle on the head. Quickly she struck two more

blows. The turtle blinked each time. Then, with a groan, he turned back to the water and swam down out of sight.

"He certainly is a nuisance," said Aunt Toolia, coming back to Warton. "Look what he's done to my umbrella. It's ruined." She put the umbrella back under the bush. "Now, as I was saying, it all started on that horrible day last week..."

As Aunt Toolia continued talking, she hopped onto the fallen sycamore tree and started for the woods across the water. Warton stayed close behind her.

"First," said Aunt Toolia, "I ran out of cinnamon fern, which I needed for some cookies I promised to bake for Gustave the woodchuck's birthday. Then I knocked over the tub in which I was dying some fringe work for the chipmunk sisters, and I discovered I had no more bloodroot with which to make more dye."

Aunt Toolia jumped off the end of the tree, and, as she began gathering more food for the fawn, Warton did the same.

"Well," said Aunt Toolia, continuing with her story, "since the best cinnamon fern and bloodroot grow in The Bog, I hurried here. I was nearly finished when a terrible scream came from up there." She pointed to some boulders on the side of a steep hill behind them. "It was a wildcat, and he was chasing the fawn. I happened to look up just as the fawn jumped from the rocks to the water. He went quickly to the island and hid behind the fallen tree, and after the wildcat gave up looking for him, I found the poor fawn just lying there—the fall was too much for his young legs. So," said Aunt Toolia, "what could I do but stay and take care of him till he got better?"

By now the two toads had all the grass and leaves and twigs they could carry, and they jumped back onto the fallen tree.

"I must say, though," said Aunt Toolia as they went along, "I had no idea how much a fawn needs to eat. It seems to be far more than I can handle, and now I'm afraid he's growing weaker."

Again they hopped off the tree and went behind the roots, where Warton set his greens beside Aunt Toolia's. The pile was nearly as big as the toads themselves, but next to the fawn it was hardly noticeable.

The fawn stirred and hungrily flicked out his tongue. The greens vanished and, although his eyes were filled with gratitude, it was plain to see he needed much more.

Without another word, Warton and Aunt Toolia started back across the tree. All night long, they made trip after trip. And bundle after bundle of leaves, twigs, and grass were set before the starving fawn. Each time, with one swift flick of his tongue, he disposed of it all.

Just at dawn, Aunt Toolia sat down to catch her breath. Before she could help herself, she was asleep. Glad to see her getting some rest, Warton continued working by himself.

"Oh, mercy!" cried Aunt Toolia when she awoke a bit later. "What have I done!" She hopped to her feet, and for the rest of the day the two toads carried greens across the tree. They didn't slow down till day was fading into night. And then a change came over the fawn.

"Look!" cried Aunt Toolia, setting down a pile of birch leaves.

Warton hurried to Aunt Toolia's side, and saw with dismay that the fawn had become so weak he could no longer even reach out his tongue. He

watched as Aunt Toolia put the leaves directly into the fawn's mouth, and he knew then that the fawn would not last much longer unless he had a great deal more to eat.

Warton could see that Aunt Toolia knew this too. Together he and Aunt Toolia looked out over the still waters of The Bog. A pale moon was beginning to rise above the hills and, overhead, bats flitted about as they gobbled up their supper of tiny insects. From far off in some distant part of The Bog there came an unearthly sound. Shrill and quivering, it carried in eerie echoes over the toads' heads to disappear into the dark woods beyond.

Aunt Toolia looked at Warton. "Dear me," she said with a shiver. "That creature sounds even more dreadful than the wildcat."

Warton nodded. Then the horrible sound came again. Suddenly Warton's eyes grew wide and he jumped up. "That isn't some terrible creature!" he cried. "That's a wood rat named Higg, and he's playing his bugle! If I can find where the rats live, they might give us enough help to feed the fawn."

"Do you think they would?" asked Aunt Toolia hopefully.

"Well, I know they're very generous," said Warton, as he jumped onto the tree. "They give presents for hardly any reason at all."

As Warton started out over the water, Aunt Toolia shouted after him, "Be careful, Warton. You'll never be in a more dangerous place!"

I n the shadowy moonlight Warton followed the sounds of the bugle. The quivering notes led him through thick mud, slimy water, and coarse grass. They led him over sharp rocks, and under rotting logs. They led him deep into the very heart of The Bog.

And then they stopped.

Warton turned his head from side to side, but not another note came. "How will I find the rats now?" he thought. "And what if I can't find my way back to Aunt Toolia?" He stood a moment, and then he decided to keep going in the direction he was headed.

Before long he came to a tree with low, spreading branches. He was about to pass beneath it when something seemed to tell him to look up. When he did a gasp escaped him. Every branch was alive with twisting and coiling snakes, and Warton shuddered at the thought of what might have happened if he had gone a few steps farther.

Then, as he looked about, he noticed a small slope nearby. "Perhaps up there," he thought, "I can see which way to go."

At the top of the slope was one lone hickory tree, very tall, with branches like bony fingers. Soon Warton was standing beneath them. There, in the bright moonlight, he had a clear view of what lay ahead. Off in the distance was yet another bog. At the bottom of the slope was a point of land that stretched out into the water. Only a few trees grew there, and scattered among them were several mounds of sticks and twigs. Then Warton saw something that made him shout with joy.

"The wood rats!" he cried.

He hurried down the slope, and the nearer the bottom he got, the more rats he saw. Where the point of land began, there were so many Warton could hardly move among them.

Most of the wood rats were gathered around four long awnings that formed an X, with a clearing in the middle. Under the awnings were many tables covered with all sorts of things. There were

double boilers and baking tins, shoes and ties, collections of pretty stones, and stacks of flowerpots. Out in the open Warton saw displays of tables and chairs, stovepipes and washtubs, and several things he had never seen before. And everywhere there were signs. Some said LIKE NEW, or PERFECT CONDITION. Others said A REAL BARGAIN, or NEEDS WORK.

Most of the wood rats were engaged in loud discussions, and each one, Warton noticed, carried a sack.

As he passed one group, a rat cried out, "Do you think I'm crazy, Morgus? For this almost perfect lunch pail you want to give only one doorknob?"

"Oh, all right," said another rat wearing a leather hat with a yellow feather. "How about a shoehorn too?"

"Now, that's more like it!" said the first rat.

Warton moved on to another group where a rat was showing a frying pan to three friends.

"Imagine!" The rat with the frying pan chuckled. "I got this from Kwill for only a pair of galoshes."

The other wood rats laughed and offered congratulations.

Everywhere Warton looked he saw wood rats happily trading one thing for another, but nowhere did he see Higg or Bundy.

He was standing beside a table filled with tiny wood carvings when he noticed a gold button hanging loosely from his sweater. He pulled it off and studied it for a moment.

"That any good?" asked a wood rat in a hoarse whisper.

"Yes," replied Warton.

The wood rat stared at Warton and seemed to be waiting for something. "Well," he said, "what would you like?"

"Oh, I'd like to know where Higg and Bundy are," said Warton.

"Fair enough," said the wood rat. "Come with me."

The wood rat led Warton far out onto the point of land. Then he stopped and pointed to a mound of sticks where a large wood rat was sitting and gazing out over the water. "There's Bundy," he said.

"Thank you very much," said Warton, heading for Bundy.

"Stop!" called the wood rat.

Warton turned around.

"Where's my button?" demanded the wood rat. "I showed you where Bundy was. Now honor your part of the bargain, and give me the button."

Warton could see the wood rat was serious, so he handed over the gold button.

The wood rat examined it carefully, then went off whistling.

Warton went straight to Bundy.

"Hello, Warton," said Bundy, grinning. "You should have been here sooner. Higg was playing his bugle to get in the mood for trading. He's gone inside now for his trading sack."

Just then Higg stepped out of one of the wood-rat homes. "Greetings, Warton," he said. "Come to do some trading?"

"No," said Warton. "I'm here because my Aunt Toolia is feeding an injured fawn at the south end of The Bog. But she needs lots of help, and I told her she could count on you wood rats for that."

"You told her the right thing, Warton," said Higg. "Come on, Bundy. Grab your trading sack, and as soon as we get some other rats we'll be off."

"Oh, you won't need your trading sacks," said Warton. "Aunt Toolia has nothing to trade."

Higg spun around and stared at Warton. "Nothing to trade?" he said, sounding disappointed. "Then we can't go."

Warton could not believe his ears. "I don't understand."

"It's simple," said Higg. "We're wood rats. And wood rats are traders. And traders don't do anything unless it's for a trade."

"Not even favors?" said Warton.

"Especially favors," replied Higg. "That's the best reason for a trade there is."

Then Bundy spoke up. "Wood rats always say one thing: It's this for that, and that for this."

"True," said Higg. "If we help your Aunt Toolia without a trade, the other rats will laugh at us, and never trade with us again."

The three stood in silence. Finally Warton said, "Aunt Toolia does have *one* thing, although it's not much good anymore."

The two wood rats were listening with rapt attention.

"Her umbrella," said Warton. "I bet she'd trade that gladly."

Higg and Bundy looked at each other, smiled, and picked up their sacks.

"Let's go, Warton," said Higg. "Bundy and I will share the umbrella, and in return she'll have the aid of *two* rats, anyway."

Although Warton was delighted to have their help, he had grave doubts that it would be enough to save the starving fawn. Nevertheless, with Higg and Bundy at his side, he started back towards the fallen sycamore tree. They were in the very midst of the trading wood rats when a horrible cry filled the air. As Warton realized what it was, an icy chill gripped his heart.

With one great bound after another, the wild-cat came screaming down the slope. He charged into the crowd of wood rats and all became pan-

demonium as they fled from his gnashing teeth and slashing claws. Tables were overturned and goods flew into the air. The cries of the rats and the howls of the wildcat made a din that was unimaginable.

Warton turned and ran until he was far out on the point of land. Then there was no place left to go, and the wildcat was coming ever closer.

"Over here, Warton!" came a shout.

Warton saw Higg standing beside a mound of sticks and pointing to a small hole. With one leap, Warton landed beside him and they hurried inside.

As they went deeper into the rat home, Warton heard the wildcat's screams overhead, and everything began to shake.

"Don't worry," said Higg. "This is a very sturdy home."

In the utter blackness Warton and Higg stood and waited until the wildcat's screams came from farther off.

"Don't move," warned Higg, "until I light a candle."

Warton wondered why Higg had said that, but when the flickering flame cast its light about he understood.

It was the most cluttered room he had ever seen. From corner to corner it was crammed with boxes and crates. Bags and sacks were scattered everywhere. Warton counted six closets and ten dressers, each one overflowing. Directly in front of him was a carton of assorted balls. On top of that was a crate of curtain rods, and on top of the curtain rods, a box of candle holders. From the ceiling hung chains and ropes, flags, lampshades, and teakettles.

"Have a seat," said Higg.

Warton glanced about. He saw straight chairs, rocking chairs, soft chairs, and hard chairs, but nowhere did he see an empty chair. Finally, he moved a jar of door keys and a bucket of argyle socks from a stuffed chair, and settled down into that.

"What a mess," said Higg.

"It *could* use some straightening up," said Warton.

"I'm talking about the wildcat situation," said Higg, disappearing behind a stack of barrels.

Warton decided to get up and look about. He squeezed his way through a long, narrow aisle, and he came upon two fat wood rats sitting on a high-backed sofa with several piles of pot holders between them. Each wore red overalls, and one had a white hat with a red flower in it.

"Hello," said one of the rats. "Who are you?"

"I'm Warton," said Warton.

"Pleased to meet you," said the rat. "My friends call me Satisfaction—because that's what a trade with me means." He pointed to the other end of the sofa. "And this is my sister, Sweet Deal."

Sweet Deal leaned forward and spoke confidentially to Warton. "We're the two best traders in the whole Bog," she said. Then she studied Warton carefully. "And right now I'm prepared to offer you a lovely popcorn popper for those hiking boots of yours."

"Hold on there, Warton," said Satisfaction. "*I'll* make that six knife, fork, and spoon sets, with most pieces having the initial *J*."

At that, Sweet Deal peered around the pot holders. "Throw in some silver polish, Satisfaction, and I'll give *you* the popper."

"You've got a deal," said Satisfaction happily.

As the two rats made their trade Warton walked off, and came upon Bundy, who was just stepping through an arched doorway.

"I'm glad to see you're safe," said Warton.

"Me too," said Bundy with a grin.

At that moment Higg appeared. "I'm afraid I've got bad news for you," he said to Warton. "They say the wildcat is still up there, and it looks as if he isn't going to leave."

"Well, I've got good news," said Bundy. "It's eating time."

"Come along, Warton," said Higg. "You may be lucky."

Warton wasn't sure what Higg meant, but he decided to go anyway. Following Higg and Bundy, he entered a long hallway. As he went along he noticed that there were many other hallways, and they all connected to the one he was in. Rats poured out of every one, and they were coming together in ever larger numbers. Young and old, big and small, they were all going in the same direction, and all were carrying something. Many had sacks with them, as did Higg and Bundy, but others had bowls, kettles, pots, pans, dishes, and trays.

Then they came to an enormous room filled with rows and rows of tables and benches. Warton watched as all about the room many of the rats set down their bowls or kettles, or whatever it was they had carried in. The other rats started to circle slowly around them.

Suddenly a shout went up, "Stew here! Get your stew here!"

And all about the room other wood rats began shouting.

"Hot hash!" cried one.

"Nuts!" shouted another. "All kinds—acorn, walnut, hazel ... "

Warton began to feel very hungry.

"Want some hot soup?" said a rat wearing a striped bandana.

Warton looked down into a big steaming kettle. "It looks delicious," he said. "I believe I will, thank you."

"Sure," said the rat. "What's your offer?"

"Offer?" said Warton. Then he overheard two rats nearby.

"One jumprope for that plate of hash," said one.

"You've got it," said the rat with the hash.

"Why, they even trade for food," thought Warton amazed. By now he was so hungry that without hesitating he pulled a gold button from his sweater and held it out. "Here," he said.

"And here's your soup," said the rat.

Warton took the bowl of soup to a table. But after the first sip he thought of the starving fawn, and then of Aunt Toolia running back and forth over the fallen tree, and he could eat no more. He looked around at all the rats. "If only they would help," he thought.

Then Higg and Bundy sat down across from him.

"The wildcat got one of our best friends tonight," said Higg sadly.

"Mullins was the nicest rat that ever lived," said Bundy.

"Mullins just couldn't run fast enough," said another rat.

"That has nothing to do with it," said a rat with a piece missing from one ear. "I'm the fastest rat here, and *I* almost got caught."

"Of course," said yet another rat. "No matter how fast a rat may be, that wildcat will always get him in the end if he runs far enough."

All the rats nodded in agreement and then were silent.

After a while one of them said, "Pass the salt, please."

Silently, the rats passed the salt from one to another.

Then the rat with the piece of ear missing spoke. "If only the wildcat would go into the Upper Bog," he said. "That would end our problem for good."

The others nodded.

Warton turned to Higg. "How would that end your problem?" he asked.

"Quicksand pools," replied Higg. "That's why no big animal ever goes there. Once they step into one, it sucks them down and they're gone forever."

Again the wood rats grew silent.

"Pass the salt," called the rat next to Warton.

As the salt passed from rat to rat, Warton's eyes

66

began to blink. It was something he did whenever he thought very hard. "I know of a way you can get the wildcat to go wherever you want," he said.

All the rats at his table stopped eating and looked at Warton. The next table did the same thing, then the next, and the next. Finally, the whole room was completely quiet.

Then a wood rat whose fur was almost white, and who looked older than the others, stood up. "Who said he knows of a way to make the wildcat go to the Upper Bog?" he asked.

Nervously, Warton stood up.

"What's your idea, toad?" said the old rat.

"I ... I can't tell you," said Warton, his voice quivering.

"What do you mean, you can't tell me?" demanded the rat.

"I can't tell you," said Warton, "because ... because ... " The words Warton wanted to say were so unlike him, he could hardly get them out. He swallowed and tried again. "I can't tell you because ... my idea has a price."

Instantly, a murmur swept through the room.

The old rat stared at Warton. "Of course it has a price," he said, his eyes gleaming, "but what is it?"

"The price is," said Warton, "that you will help my Aunt Toolia feed a starving fawn. They are where the fallen sycamore tree lies over the water."

The old toad looked at Warton for several moments. Then he spoke. "Come here, toad, and we will bargain."

Warton crossed the room on shaking legs, and sat down. Then the toad and the wood rat began talking in hushed tones. Everyone tried to hear what the two were saying, but only the smallest snatches of conversation could be heard.

"…by noon tomorrow," the old wood rat whispered.

" … enough food for a week," came Warton's voice.

The trading went on for some time. Then the old rat stood up, and addressed the room in a loud voice. "I have heard the toad's idea, and I must say it is very strange indeed. But it now looks as if the wildcat will not leave till he has eaten us all, so we'd better give it a try." He looked at Warton. "Toad, it's a trade!"

All at once the room was in an uproar. The wood rats were so excited at the prospect of being free of the terrible wildcat, they shouted till the walls shook.

Far into the night, unusual activities occurred down in the wood-rat homes. Discussions were held, clothing was gathered, special equipment was found, and races were run in the long hallway.

Just past midnight a wood rat came running into the huge dining room where Warton sat with Higg, Bundy, and twelve other carefully selected wood rats.

"The wildcat's asleep," said the rat breathlessly. "He's in the cottonwood tree where the point of land begins!"

Warton looked at the rats. "We'd better hurry," he said, "if we're to be ready when he wakes up."

Warton, Higg, Bundy, and the twelve wood rats filed out of the dining hall. Higg, who was the only rat carrying a sack, led the way. They went up a narrow passageway and stepped outside into the night. In the clear sky the stars twinkled and the moon hung low over the trees. The air was cool and the chirping of crickets was everywhere.

Stealthily, Warton and the wood rats made their way through the wet grass till they came to the cottonwood. Fear showed on every face as they stared at the wildcat sprawled across a thick limb.

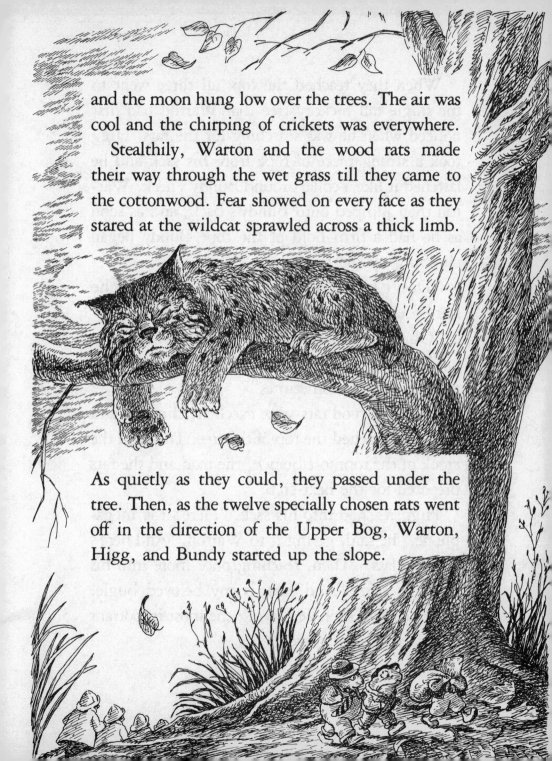

As quietly as they could, they passed under the tree. Then, as the twelve specially chosen rats went off in the direction of the Upper Bog, Warton, Higg, and Bundy started up the slope.

When they reached the top, all three went to the single tall hickory tree that Warton had first noticed when he was searching for the rats. Higg took a strong piece of rope from his sack and he fastened it like a collar around Bundy's neck. Warton then jumped onto Bundy's back, and as soon as he had a firm hold of the rope Bundy began climbing up the tree.

"Don't be afraid," whispered Higg, as he started up, too.

"Oh, I'm not worried," said Warton.

"I meant Bundy," said Higg. "High places make him faint sometimes."

The two wood rats were excellent climbers and they soon reached the top of the tree. There, in the crook of the topmost branch, the toad and the rats prepared for the next step.

Higg reached into his sack. "Here's the megaphone," he said, giving it to Warton. "And here's the spyglass." Then, reaching once more into his sack, he said, "And here is my beloved bugle. With it I will soon be playing the most important notes I have ever played."

Warton looked with satisfaction at the things Higg had set out. "Now," he said, "when the sun rises, we can start our plan."

Higg and Bundy nodded and sat down to wait.

Warton too sat down. And as he looked out over The Bog, he thought about how hungry the fawn must be, how weary Aunt Toolia must be, and how terrible it must be to lose one friend after another, as Higg and Bundy had.

Before he knew it, the stars began to dim. The sky turned from black to blue. And beyond the eastern hills the blazing edge of a new sun appeared. Its bright rays brought reds and yellows to the leaves that floated on the waters, and its warmth created gentle breezes which swayed the golden grass along the shore.

It was time. Warton, Higg, and Bundy stood up.

Warton put the megaphone to his mouth. He took a deep breath. "Wake up, you wildcat!" he said. His voice, magnified many times, rained down on The Bog.

The wildcat, asleep in the cottonwood, gave a start. His eyes popped open, and his head turned in all directions.

Again Warton spoke into the megaphone. "Wake up, you lazy wildcat! Wake up and meet a rat that is so fast you will never catch him, no matter how far you chase him!"

The wildcat's head was turning in all directions, and he was beginning to snarl.

"Look towards the path," said Warton.

The wildcat snapped his head around. Then a look of complete shock came over him, and he hooked his claws into the bark as if to keep from falling out of the tree. He stared unbelievingly at a spot far up the path. There, standing on a rotted stump, a rat wearing a yellow rain slicker and a yellow hat was sticking his tongue out at him.

"Better not try to catch him, wildcat!" shouted Warton. "He's too fast for you!"

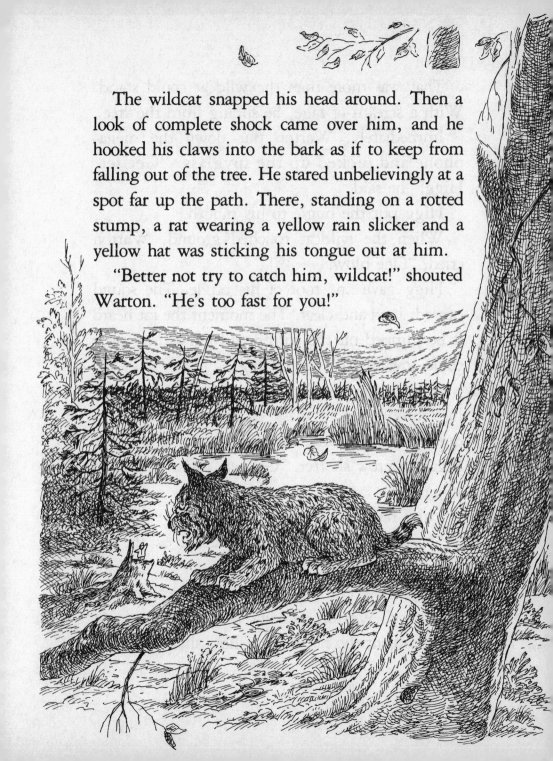

That was more than the wildcat could stand. With a scream of rage, he sprang from the tree.

Immediately, Warton put down the megaphone and picked up the spyglass. "Get set, Higg!" he said.

Higg put the bugle to his mouth.

When the wildcat touched ground, Warton cried, "One blow!"

Higg gave one toot of his bugle. The sound carried, loud and clear. The moment the rat heard it he jumped off the stump and ran as fast as he could towards the Upper Bog.

High in the tree, Warton watched the proceedings through the spyglass. At first the wildcat was quite far behind the rat, but then the distance began to grow shorter. "Get set," Warton said to Higg again.

Higg raised his bugle once more.

"Now, two blows!" said Warton, as the rat rounded a corner.

Higg blew two loud toots. They were so sour and raspy, Warton couldn't help but wince. At that moment the rat in the yellow slicker was out

76

of the wildcat's sight. When he heard the bugle notes he jumped behind a rock. At that exact time, farther along the path, another rat, who was also dressed in a yellow slicker and hat, jumped out from behind a log.

When the wildcat rounded the corner he saw only the second rat running far ahead of him up the path. Appearing a bit bewildered he roared angrily, and ran even faster.

Warton let out a cry. "It's working! The wildcat thinks it's the same rat! Now, just like the salt passing from one to the other in your dining room, those rats will lead the wildcat all the way to the Upper Bog."

Many of the leaves had fallen from the trees, so Warton had a perfect view of the chase. And each time the wildcat got too close to one rat, he would have Higg blow an extra toot on his bugle, and the next rat would take up the chase. All the rats had been chosen for their great speed, so it was easy for them to keep ahead of the wildcat for the short distance each one had to run.

Finally, it was time for the most important part of the chase, and Higg blew twelve notes on the bugle. When the last note died away, rat number eleven dove into a hole just before a row of brambles.

A moment later the wildcat came racing down the path. He looked left and right. Then, on the other side of the brambles, he saw the now familiar sight of a rat in a yellow slicker. The wildcat shook his head in confusion. Then, with a scream, he charged into the brambles. His eyes remained fixed on the rat who, to his amazement, was not running at all—he just seemed to be waiting.

Suddenly the wildcat burst out of the brambles. He gave a great leap towards the rat, then stopped short. He was in the middle of a pool of quicksand. He screamed and roared, but it did no good.

The rat on the other side of the quicksand let out a whoop of joy, and started running back towards the wood rats' homes.

High in the hickory tree, Warton picked up the megaphone. "It's all over!" he yelled. "The wildcat won't bother anyone anymore!"

Down below, the rats, laughing and shouting, streamed out of their homes. Through his spyglass, Warton saw the white-haired old rat point to the south, and, all at the same time, the rats started running in the direction of the fallen sycamore tree.

Warton sighed with relief as he watched them go. Then, wondering if perhaps he could see Aunt Toolia from his high perch, he trained the spyglass in her direction. But a rise of land stood in his way, and he turned back to the Upper Bog. As he did so, the spyglass fell in line with an open field not far from the quicksand. Beyond the tall grass there, a few scraggly apple trees grew. And under one of the trees Warton noticed a large animal— an animal with a broad spread of antlers.

"A deer!" he exclaimed.

Higg and Bundy, who were waiting anxiously to climb down out of the tree, looked at him.

"There's a deer over in the field," explained

Warton. "He might be looking for the fawn. We've got to go over there!"

"We can't," said Higg. "We promised to feed the fawn as soon as the wildcat was in the quicksand—and a bargain is a bargain."

Bundy nodded.

Warton knew there was no sense in arguing with the rats. So the moment they were back on the ground, he told Higg and Bundy to explain to Aunt Toolia where he was going. Then he hurried off for the open field.

He was not far from the quicksand when he heard a movement in the underbrush. Looking around, he was startled to catch a glimpse of reddish-gray fur passing behind some grapevines.

"If I didn't know better," said Warton, "I'd say that was the wildcat. But that's impossible. I saw him myself—he's in the quicksand."

Warton started off again, with an unsettled feeling deep inside him. Suddenly, he stopped. He could not go any farther until he knew for certain. He turned towards the quicksand. He crossed a tiny stream, and there was the bramble thicket. Warton could see quite clearly where the wildcat had smashed through it in his chase after the wood rats.

He had worked his way deep into the brambles, and was about to step out the other side when he felt a soft squishing under one foot. He looked down and saw moist sand sliding like thick syrup over his boot. Then he felt a powerful downward pull. It took all his strength to get back on solid ground.

"It's the quicksand!" he gasped.

Warton looked out over the pool. Most of it was covered with leaves, but here and there patches of quicksand showed through, looking as clean and smooth as cake batter. Nowhere did he see the wildcat. "The quicksand must have pulled him under," he said.

Just as he was leaving, his eye fell on the mucky banks at the other side of the pool. There, in the soft mud beneath a low branch, he saw several footprints. They were very deep, very wide, and ... very catlike.

"The wildcat has escaped!" cried Warton. "He climbed out onto that branch, and now he's free to go after the rats! When he finds them, he'll find Aunt Toolia and the fawn too! I've got to warn them!"

Warton spun around and hurried towards the open field as fast as he could. When he reached it he was relieved to see that the deer was still there, resting under one of the apple trees. He hopped through the high grass as fast as he could. But then, just as he drew near the trees, the deer began to trot off.

Warton cried out loudly, "Wait!"

The deer stopped, and with sad eyes looked all about. "Who said that?" he demanded. "I've no time for games, wherever you are. I must keep searching for my young one."

Warton gave several great leaps, and at last he stood before the big buck. "That's just why I came here," he gasped. "I know where he is!"

The deer gave a start. He lowered his head till he was looking straight into Warton's eyes. "*What did you say?*"

Warton explained about the fawn, Aunt Toolia, the wood rats, and the wildcat.

The buck's face was grave. "Hop on," he said when Warton was finished, "and hold on tightly."

Warton jumped onto the deer's head, and as

soon as he had a firm hold of the antlers the deer went bounding off. The wind whistled past him as they sailed over rocks and logs, and the ground became a blur as it slipped beneath the deer's thundering hooves.

They soon passed the point of land where the wood rats lived, and then the tree where Warton had seen all the snakes. They crashed through thickets and tore up skunk cabbages. Then Warton shouted, "There it is!" He pointed towards the fallen sycamore tree still some distance away.

The deer took the shortest route possible—he plunged into the water, which turned out to be rather shallow. It barely touched his stomach as he pushed ahead.

As they got closer to the sycamore tree, Warton saw that it was teeming with wood rats. Two endless lines of rats ran back and forth across the long trunk. One line carried little bundles of twigs, grasses, leaves, and water plants. The other was going back for more.

"We're in luck," said Warton. "The wildcat hasn't found them."

Hardly had he spoken when a streak of reddish gray appeared at the top of the boulders. An angry cry carried to the far ends of The Bog as the wildcat clawed at the air with one paw.

The terrified rats dashed behind the upturned roots as the roaring wildcat jumped from boulder to boulder and onto the fallen sycamore. As the wildcat made his way along the tree trunk, the deer gave a loud snort and plowed through the water with all his might. The water splashed over Warton, and he realized with a shock that the deer, in his anger, had forgotten he was there. Now he clung to the antlers more tightly than before.

When the wildcat saw the deer coming at him, he drew back his lips. His yellow teeth glistened in the sunlight. He worked his claws against the bark and gave a throaty growl.

The deer put his head down and charged, but the wildcat didn't wait. With a hiss, he sprang into the air and landed on the deer's back.

The deer, tossing his head back and forth, tried to catch the wildcat with his antlers, but the wildcat was too close to his head. Warton, holding on for his life, found himself looking straight into the wildcat's eyes.

The wildcat blinked with surprise when he saw the toad. For a moment the two stared at each other, and as they stared the many terrible things the wildcat had done passed through Warton's mind. Then Warton said under his breath, "This may be the last thing I ever do." Suddenly he reached out and yanked the wildcat's long whiskers as hard as he could.

With a loud scream, the wildcat jumped backwards.

Instantly the deer snapped his head around, and this time the wildcat was within reach of his antlers. The wildcat went flying through the air, landing in the water with a splash. Before he could catch his breath, the deer pushed him under with his sharp hooves. Then the deer quickly turned, and, when the wildcat popped up, kicked him hard with his powerful hind legs.

With that the wildcat had had enough. Without a sound he swam to dry ground, and, not looking back once, slunk over the boulders and vanished into the woods.

"I don't believe he'll ever come back here," said Warton.

The deer appeared startled at Warton's voice. "I'm afraid I forgot you were up there," he said. "Are you all right?"

"I'm as fine as can be," said Warton, looking at the three long whiskers he was holding.

As the deer waded to the back side of the little island, the rats were all shouting excitedly. Then they grew quiet as he climbed out of the water. The deer lowered his head and Warton jumped off.

Aunt Toolia was standing beside the fawn. Behind her was a huge pile of food. Warton noticed that the fawn's belly, for the first time, was round and full.

"Warton!" cried Aunt Toolia, her face beaming. "Thank goodness you're safe!" She went and stood beside him. "You certainly were right about the wood rats," she said. "They're wonderful. Although," she added with a glance toward Higg and Bundy, "when those two said I owed them my umbrella, I must say I was a bit surprised. But since it's no good to me now anyway, I gave it to them gladly."

Warton saw the bent umbrella lying beside Higg's sack. He was about to explain to Aunt Toolia about the trade, but just then the big buck caught his eye. Warton watched as he tenderly gave the fawn's tiny nose a lick with his tongue. Immediately the fawn's face lit up, and his tail began to wag furiously.

"He'll be fine in a couple of days," said Aunt Toolia. "His leg will mend nicely now that he has plenty of food, and as long as he gets lots of rest."

"You must need some rest too," said the deer to Aunt Toolia, "and I would like to repay you somehow."

Every wood rat came to attention.

"This is going to be some trade," said Higg to Bundy.

Aunt Toolia looked at the deer. "Why, I don't

want anything at all," she said. "I'm just happy as can be knowing that everything turned out all right."

A gasp arose from the wood rats. They looked at each other, stunned.

"Did I hear correctly?" said the white-haired old wood rat.

"What kind of a trade is that?" groaned Sweet Deal.

"I would have asked for free rides for a week," said Kwill.

"Six weeks at least," said another wood rat.

"I would have asked for all his old antlers," said Satisfaction.

Then the wood rats, all excitedly discussing what they would have traded, began filing across the fallen tree. Higg and Bundy were the last to leave.

"Well, Warton," said Higg, as he threw his sack over his back, "it's been a pleasure doing business with you. And if you're ever in The Bog again, be sure to stop and say hello."

Warton nodded as Bundy leaned close and whispered, "You're a good trader all right, Warton, but your Aunt Toolia doesn't know the first thing about it. Perhaps you could give her a few pointers."

With that, Higg and Bundy followed after the wood rats.

The big buck looked at Warton and Aunt

Toolia. "Thank you for all you've done," he said. "Now you must be eager to go back to your own homes. I'm sure I can feed the young one till he's strong enough to return to his mother. She's been worried sick, but when she sees him I'm sure she'll get better right away."

Warton and Aunt Toolia said good-bye to the fawn and the big deer. Then they both hopped onto the fallen sycamore tree.

"Why, look at this," said Aunt Toolia, point-ing down at her feet.

Warton was surprised to see Aunt Toolia's bent umbrella lying across the trunk of the tree.

"Well," said Aunt Toolia, picking it up, "either those rats forgot it or they just didn't want it in the first place."

"Hmmm," said Warton, "I wonder which one it was?"

Then, as a flight of geese honked noisily overhead, the two toads trudged off towards Aunt Toolia's home.